Mystery
of the
Melodies
From Mars

Bethany House Books by
Bill Myers

Bloodhounds, Inc.
CHILDREN'S MYSTERY SERIES

The Ghost of KRZY
The Mystery of the Invisible Knight
Phantom of the Haunted Church
Invasion of the UFOs
Fangs for the Memories
The Case of the Missing Minds
The Secret of the Ghostly Hot Rod
I Want My Mummy
The Curse of the Horrible Hair Day
The Scam of the Screwball Wizards
Mystery of the Melodies From Mars

Nonfiction

The Dark Side of the Supernatural
Hot Topics, Tough Questions

Bill Myers' Web site: *www.BillMyers.com*

BloodHounds, INC.

11

Mystery of the Melodies From Mars

Bill Myers

with DAVE WIMBISH

BETHANY HOUSE PUBLISHERS
MINNEAPOLIS, MINNESOTA 55438

Published by Bethany House Publishers
A Ministry of Bethany Fellowship International
11400 Hampshire Avenue South
Bloomington, Minnesota 55438
www.bethanyhouse.com

Printed in the United States of America by
Bethany Press International, Bloomington, Minnesota 55438

Library of Congress Cataloging-in-Publication Data

Myers, Bill, 1953–
    Mystery of the melodies from Mars / by Bill Myers ; with Dave Wimbish.
        p.   cm. — (BloodHounds, Inc.)
Summary: A rash of burglaries hits Midvale at the same time as the rock band Spice Army arrives to give a concert and the oscillating audio spectroscope starts picking up strange signals from outer space.
    ISBN 0-7642-2623-1
    [1. Brothers and sisters—Fiction. 2. Rock music—Fiction. 3. Christian life—Fiction. 4. Mystery and detective stories.] I. Wimbish, David. II. Title.
    PZ7.M98234 Myw 2002
    [Fic]—dc21   2001007698

This one's for Molly

BILL MYERS is a youth worker, creative writer, and film director who co-created the "McGee and Me!" book and video series; his work has received over forty national and international awards. His many books include THE INCREDIBLE WORLDS OF WALLY MCDOOGLE series; his teen books: *Hot Topics, Tough Questions; Faith Encounter;* and *Forbidden Doors;* as well as his adult novels: *When the Last Leaf Falls; Eli;* and the trilogy *Blood of Heaven, Threshold,* and *Fire of Heaven.*

Contents

Abstain from all appearance of evil.

1 Thessalonians 5:22

1

The Case Begins

THURSDAY, 17:12 PDST

"You do have the tickets, don't you?" Melissa asked.

"Of course I do," Sean said. "They're right here in my—" He reached into his shirt pocket but came up empty. "I mean, right here in my—" He tried his pants pocket and found three Snickers wrappers, a crumbled chocolate chip cookie, one bent baseball card, two paper clips, a half-chewed pencil, seven pennies . . . but no tickets.

"Sean," Melissa groaned, "please don't tell me you lost them. I really want to see this concert."

Melissa and her brother were dropping off Slobs, their bloodhound, at Doc's house. Then they were heading over to a concert featuring the popular rock band Spice Army. The group was performing a series of concerts for Midvale's annual Summer Festival. Melissa had been a fan of theirs since she heard their hit song "Artful Moosey." (She had no idea what the title meant, but that was okay. Nobody else did, either.)

"Yes, sir, it's a great evening for a concert," Melissa said, folding her arms across her chest. "*If* you happen to have tickets, that is."

"Don't worry," Sean said. "I know I have them somewhere." He reached into his other pants pocket and—"Ah, here we go." He pulled out two crumpled tickets stuck together by something pink and gooey. "Cool!" he exclaimed. "I wondered what I did with that bubble gum." He pulled the tickets apart, scraped off the gum, and popped it into his mouth. "Mmm." He smiled. "Still a little flavor left."

"And I bet all that lint gives it an extra little zing," Melissa added.

Sean stopped chewing, then nodded and started again. "I think you might have a point." Then, handing the gooey tickets over to her, he asked, "You want to try? There's still some left."

Melissa rolled her eyes, trying not to gag.

"Honestly, Sean, sometimes I think you—"

KA-BLAMMMM!

The blast was so powerful that it knocked them off their feet. A moment later broken glass was raining down on the sidewalk all around them.

"What was that?" Melissa gasped.

"I don't know."

Slowly they rose to their feet, shaking tiny glass fragments out of their hair.

"Where did it come from?" Sean asked.

"Right there." Melissa pointed. "From Doc's house!"

Sean turned. "Wow!"

It was quite a sight. Every window in her upstairs laboratory had been blown out.

"Come on!" Sean shouted. "She might be hurt!"

"I'm right behind you!" Melissa yelled. "Come on, Slobs!"

Apparently, the big dog had other ideas. She tilted her head as if listening to something very painful and let out a long, mournful . . .

"AROOOOOOOOOOOOOO!"

. . . then tucked her tail between her legs and raced off toward home.

"What's with her?" Sean shouted.

"Beats me," Melissa yelled. "Let's go!"

They arrived at Doc's front door. Strangely enough, it wasn't locked, so they pushed it open, ran inside, and started up the steps to her laboratory.

"Doc!" Sean yelled. "Are you okay? Doc?"

"She can't hear you!" Melissa shouted. "You know that."

"Oh, right."

Doc, as you probably know by now, cannot hear or speak. She was born that way. But her disability never held her back. She was a brilliant scientist and inventor (though most of the time her inventions were anything but brilliant. They often backfired in the most amazing ways). But more importantly, she was Sean and Melissa's friend, and she often used her whacked-out inventions to help their detective agency, Bloodhounds, Inc.

Sean ran into Doc's laboratory with Melissa right behind.

By the looks of things, Doc was all right. No

broken body parts, no cuts, no bruises. Instead, she sat at—what was that? It looked like an electric organ, except that it had all kinds of knobs, switches, and flashing lights attached to it.

Apparently, she wasn't even aware of the explosion. Instead, with her eyes closed in rapture, she was banging away on the keyboard like Elton John. But for all her banging, the keys weren't making a sound.

"What do you think she's doing?" Sean asked.

Melissa shrugged. "I have no idea."

"Whatever it is," Sean said, looking toward Doc's shattered windows, "she'd better be more careful." He walked over and tapped Doc on the shoulder.

Doc's eyes flew open in startled surprise. When she saw Sean and Melissa standing there, an embarrassed smile spread across her face. She pulled her hands away from the keyboard and signed, *Hi, guys. What brings you here?*

"The explosion!" Sean said. He faced her squarely while he talked so she could read his lips.

Explosion? Doc answered in sign language. *What explosion?*

13

"That explosion!" Sean said, pointing to the jagged shards of glass that still hung in Doc's laboratory windows.

Doc gasped and clasped her hands to her face.

Sean stepped to one of the computer keyboards and typed, *I guess you must have played that last note a little too loud, which is funny because that thing wasn't making a sound when we came in here.*

Melissa pointed to the strange instrument. "What is it?" she asked. "Some kind of piano for deaf people?"

Doc chuckled in spite of herself. She reached for the computer terminal and typed, *This is an oscillating audio spectroscope. It's probably just like the one your dad has down at the radio station . . . except that I've made a few minor modifications.*

Melissa shook her head and signed, *I think I'd know if Dad had one of these. What does it do?*

Doc turned back to the computer keyboard and typed, *Like I said, I've made a few modifications to this one. I'm using it to look for life in outer space.*

"Life in outer space!" Sean and Melissa said at the same time.

That's right, Doc typed. *Life in outer space.*

She explained that she had just received a contract from NASA to assist the agency in its search for extraterrestrial intelligence.

What the spectroscope does, she typed, *is use an ultra-high frequency to send a message into outer space, and then wait for an answer.*

"What kind of message?" Sean asked.

Doc shrugged and typed, *"Hello from earth. How are you? How are things on your planet?" You know, stuff like that.*

"Wow!" Melissa exclaimed.

Doc resumed typing. *Then, if there's somebody out there and they answer us, this machine will pick it up.*

Sean was still struggling to learn how to sign, but he knew a few sentences, including one he used far too often: *Can I try it?*

Doc frowned. She didn't think it was a very good idea. It seemed every time Sean touched one of her inventions, disaster followed.

Melissa was obviously thinking the same

thing. "I don't know, Sean. Remember what happened when—"

"Yeah, yeah, I'll be careful," he said. "Thanks, Doc!"

Before she could protest, he stepped to the machine's keyboard and began punching keys, playing the only song he knew: "Louie, Louie." (Or was it "Chopsticks"? With Sean's talent it all sounded the same.)

"See," he said as he finished, "nothing happened. Nothing at all."

The guy wouldn't have been so sure if he'd seen what was going on around the neighborhood just outside the lab. First there were . . .

KA-BLAM! KA-BLAM! KA-BLAM!

. . . the Johnsons' windows. Followed by the . . .

KA-BLOOWIE! KA-BLOOWIE!
KA-BLOOWIE!

. . . Ortegas' windows. And finally, not to be outdone, there were the . . .

KA-POOIE! KA-POOIE! KA-POOIE!

. . . Browns'.

But that was just for starters. Next, the

nearest streetlight suddenly . . .

KA-POW!

. . . disintegrated, sending a shower of glass to the ground. Then . . .

KA-SPLASH!

. . . there went Henrietta Dudley's aquarium, spilling thirty-five gallons of water onto her brand-new carpet, along with a thousand dollars' worth of rare and exotic fish. Needless to say, this sent Henrietta running around her living room, screaming and scooping up the wriggling creatures. "I'll save you!" she cried. "I'll save you!"

And her husband, right behind her, was shouting, "Put 'em in the toilet! Put 'em in the toilet!" (Well, where else are you going to find that much water in a hurry?)

And finally, there was Bill Putka, who just happened to be driving past when suddenly his windshield . . .

*KA-RACKKKKK*ed!

. . . into a giant spider web of broken glass.
"Help!" he yelled. "I can't see! I can't see!"

17

He slammed on the brake. At least, that's what he meant to do. But in his excitement, he missed and hit the gas pedal. The car shot across the street, up over the curb, and into a fire hydrant, where it sent a stream of water high into the Midvale sky—which, sadly, for some strange reason, caused all the toilets in the neighborhood to start flushing, including, that's right . . . Henrietta Dudley's.

Glug . . . glug . . . glug . . .

Not far away, Channel 38's intrepid reporter, Rafael Ruelas, was up in the air giving an afternoon traffic report from Cloud Copter Cam:

"Concert goers are already starting to arrive in Midvale and—wait a minute, it looks like something big is happening over near Fourth Street. Stay tuned while we investigate for a live eyewitness report."

Meanwhile, back in Doc's laboratory, Sean yawned and looked at his watch. "See, I told you nothing was going to happen if I played this thing!"

"I guess you were right," Melissa said. "For once."

"I'm always right," Sean snorted. "Anyway, we'd better get going or we're going to be late for the concert."

Melissa looked around at the broken windows. "Maybe we should stay and help Doc clean up this mess," she said.

Don't be silly, Doc typed. *Domesticus will take care of it. You two go on.*

"Domesticus!" Melissa exclaimed. "Your robot?"

Doc nodded.

"But what if he does something crazy again?" Melissa asked. "Like deciding to shave the neighbor's cat?" (See *Fangs for the Memories* for all the hairy details.)

Doc smiled and shooed them away. *He doesn't do that kind of thing anymore*, she signed. *You two go on and enjoy yourselves.*

"Well, if you say so," Melissa said. But the young detectives had barely started toward the door when . . .

BRRRRRP!

. . . Sean's cell phone rang.

He threw a look to Melissa, knowing exactly what she was thinking: *Can't you let it go, just this once?*

BRRRRRP!

He wanted to ignore it—he really did. And next time he would. But for now, he opened the lid and spoke: "Bloodhounds, Incorporated."

He paused a moment, then answered, "Yes, this is Sean Hunter." Another pause. "Yes, I see." Another one. "Yes, I see." And another. "Yes, I see."

(If he said "Yes, I see" one more time, Melissa was going to punch him in the nose.)

Lucky for him, he didn't.

Unlucky for her, he said something even worse.

"Yes, sir, we will be there in fifteen minutes." Then he hung up.

"Sean!" Melissa whined. "Don't tell me we can't go to the concert."

"I'm sorry," he said, "but it looks like we can't go to the concert."

"I asked you not to tell me that!" Melissa complained. Then, with a deep sigh she asked, "Okay, where are we going?"

"Where else—" he grinned—"but to the scene of the crime!"

2

Midvale:
Crime City, USA?

THURSDAY, 17:58 PDST

As Sean and Melissa hurried out of Doc's house, they saw the Channel 38 Cloud Copter hovering a short distance away.

"Whadd'ya think's going on?" Melissa asked.

"Who knows." Sean shrugged. "But whatever it is, it doesn't have anything to do with us."

BRRRRRRRP!

It was Sean's cell phone again. He answered, "Bloodhounds, Incorporated. Yes, ma'am. A burglary? We'll, we're kind of busy—" he looked at his watch—"but we'll try to squeeze you in."

"Who was that?" Melissa asked.

"It was . . ."

BRRRRRRRRRP!

"This is getting ridiculous!" he said. "Bloodhounds, Incorporated. Yes, sir . . . a burglary, you say?" He put his hand over the mouthpiece and whispered to his sister, "It's another burglary."

He turned back to the phone. "I'm afraid we can't come right away. We have two other burglaries before we can get to yours. But we'll try."

He sighed as he folded the phone and snapped it back into its case. "Three burglaries in one evening," he said. "I've got a strange feeling about this."

"Feeling?" Melissa asked.

"Yes," Sean said, rubbing his chin in thought. "I have a strange feeling that something unusual is going on in Midvale."

Melissa broke out laughing and clapped him on the back. "No wonder you're such a great detective," she giggled. "Nothing can get past you."

"Thank you," Sean said proudly. "Thank you very much."

THURSDAY, 18:04 PDST

At the amphitheater, applause rippled through the crowd as the stage curtain opened ever so slightly, then closed. False alarm. Then, thirty seconds later, the curtain swung open wide. The crowd went crazy as Spice Army roared onto the stage with their ear-splitting rock 'n' roll.

These guys could play! Especially the keyboard player. He danced around, banging those keys on that . . . er . . . whatever it was . . . for all he was worth. First with his hands behind his back, next with his elbow, and after that with his feet. Funny, though, the organ, or whatever it was, didn't seem to be making a sound. Maybe it was drowned out by the screaming guitars or the screaming singers or the screaming fans. Maybe it was all of the above.

Or maybe not . . .

Meanwhile, Doc sat staring at the various

gauges on her spectrograph. She knew she was being rather silly. After all, NASA has been looking for extraterrestrial life for nearly fifty years. It wasn't likely that she was going to get a message from space the very first time she tried.

She yawned and stood up, feeling very tired. She'd been working too hard. She started to walk away and then stopped. She thought she saw something out of the corner of her eye. Had that light on the spectrograph blinked?

She stood and waited, but nothing happened. Must have been her imagination.

She turned to go and . . .

There it was again!

No doubt about it this time. That light was definitely blinking! Again . . . and again . . . and again!

Somebody, somewhere, out there in space, was talking to her!

THURSDAY, 18:15 PDST

"Hello, Mr. Petersen." Sean stuck out his hand. "I'm Sean Hunter, and this is my sis . . . er . . . associate, Melissa."

Mr. Petersen, a tall, thin man of about sixty, with a sharp nose and bushy white eyebrows, looked down at them over the top of his glasses. "So you are Bloodhounds, Incorporated," he said. "You two seem kind of young to be detectives."

Sean cleared his throat. "I assure you, we know our business, and—"

Mr. Petersen waved for him to stop. "Oh, I've heard how good you are," he said. "That's why I called you. Now, follow me, and I'll show what the thieves took from my store."

Mr. Petersen, who was owner of Petersen's Books, led them down a maze of crowded aisles until they reached a section marked "Study Guides and Textbooks."

There were several empty spaces on one of the shelves—places where books should have been but weren't.

Sean gave Mr. Petersen a curious look. "You mean, the burglar didn't steal money?" he asked.

Mr. Petersen shook his head. "Nope. Far as I can tell, he never touched the cash register." He pointed toward the back of the store. "I've got some pretty expensive items back there in the Rare Books section, but he didn't touch those, either. All he took were—"

"Textbooks?" Melissa finished his sentence.

"That's right. Textbooks." Mr. Petersen pulled a piece of paper from his shirt pocket, unfolded it, and adjusted his glasses so he could read. "And not just *any* textbooks. Listen to some of these titles." He began to read from his list.

"*Crazy About Calculus . . . The Migration Patterns of the American Slug . . . Having Fun With Quantum Physics . . . The Adverb Is Your Friend . . .*"

He stopped reading and folded the paper, putting it back in his pocket. "You get the idea," he said. "Do you know how long I've had some of those books on my shelf?"

Sean started to answer, but he didn't have a chance.

"Years!" the old man said. "Not only couldn't I sell them . . . I couldn't give them away! What kind of strange person would break into a store

28

to steal books like these?"

"Very strange," Sean answered.

"But I don't understand," Melissa said. "If you're not upset about what was stolen, why do you want to hire us?"

Mr. Petersen looked around to make sure nobody was listening to their conversation.

"Because," he whispered, "I don't like the idea that somebody was in my store last night after it was closed. I mean . . . who knows? If they broke in here once, they could do it again. Maybe this was just a trial run."

"A trial run?" Sean asked. "What do you mean by that?"

Mr. Petersen shrugged his shoulders. "Maybe someone was practicing on my store for something bigger later on." He pushed his glasses up higher on his nose. "Anyway, catch the person who broke into my store, and I'll make it well worth your time."

"Yes, sir," Sean said. "Well, we'd better get busy."

"Certainly," said Mr. Petersen. "I'll be in my office if you need me."

With that, the two went to work. Melissa

began dusting for fingerprints as Sean started looking for any other clues.

"I can't imagine why anyone would steal books like those," Melissa said.

"Me either," Sean agreed. "You'd have to be a real weirdo."

"Or a brain," Melissa said. "Somebody real smart like, oh, I don't know, like . . ."

"Spalding," Sean said.

"Well, now that you mention it, yeah, someone like Spalding."

"No," Sean said. "He's right there."

Melissa turned to look where Sean was pointing. Sure enough, there was Spalding, hurrying past the store.

Spalding, as you no doubt know, was proud of being the smartest kid at Midvale Middle School. He knew everything there was to know, and he was more than happy to tell you about it—sometimes for hours. Or at least it seemed that way. What made it even worse was that Spalding was also the richest kid in town, and he didn't mind letting you know about that, either.

As usual, he was flanked by his friends KC, the roughest, toughest girl in town, and Bear, who got his nickname because he was big, like a bear (and almost as smart). But what was not so usual was that Spalding was wearing pants about five sizes too big, a ripped, sleeveless T-shirt, and a giant chain that hung from his pocket.

Sean and Melissa ran out of the store, calling after them. "Hey, guys, where you going?"

The group turned to them without stopping.

"We're on our way to the Spice Army concert," KC shouted, "and we've gotta hurry 'cause we're really late."

"But you went yesterday, didn't you?" Sean asked.

"And we'll be back tomorrow," Bear said, " 'cause they're the best!" Then, turning to Spalding, he said, "Show 'em your new tattoo!"

Spalding slowed to a stop. Even though he was late, he was never too late when it came to showing off. Proudly, he turned his arm to reveal a crudely drawn dragon carrying a dagger.

"It's just like the one their drummer has," Bear explained.

"Cool!" Melissa heard herself say (even though she was really kind of disgusted by it). "Where'd you get it?"

"Dibbadobba babba labna," Spalding answered.

"What?" Melissa asked. "Is that like pig Latin?"

Spalding sighed, took a deep breath, and said, "Uh seb . . . Dibbadobba babba labna."

Sean and Melissa both shook their heads.

"I can't understand a word you're saying," Sean said.

Spalding opened his mouth wide to reveal that he had a stud in his tongue. It was even monogrammed with a big *S*.

"Spalding!" Melissa shrieked. "You got your tongue pierced!"

"Nab ab didna!" Spalding reached into his mouth and pulled the stud off his tongue. "It is simply a clip-on," he said. "Here, would you like to examine it more closely?"

Melissa shuddered and took a step backward. "Uh, no thanks."

"Wow! A clip-on tongue stud!" Sean said. "That's gotta hurt!"

"It most certainty does," Spalding agreed. "However, it is certainly worth it."

"That's not his first," KC chimed in. "He lost one already."

"I did not lose it," Spalding said indignantly. "Somebody—"

"I know, I know," KC laughed. "Somebody stole it. It's easy to understand why someone would want to steal a clip-on tongue stud with your initial on it!"

"Regardless of what you think, that is precisely what occurred!"

"I'm sure it is," Melissa said. "But, Spalding, do you really want to go around looking like . . . like some punk-rocker?"

Spalding laughed. "Don't be concerned. I certainly do not take any of this seriously. It is simply a source of amusement. Incidentally, I was under the assumption you two were also attending this evening's concert."

"We were," Sean said, "but then we had to come over here to investigate a burglary. Somebody stole a bunch of textbooks."

"Textbooks?" KC asked. "Why would anybody want to steal textbooks?"

"That's exactly what we're trying to figure out," Melissa said. "Got any ideas?"

33

"I really cannot imagine why anyone would choose to purloin textbooks," Spalding said.

Melissa and Sean exchanged glances. *Purloin?* "You mean, 'steal'?" they asked.

Spalding nodded. (It was nearly impossible to have a conversation with the guy without having a dictionary handy.) He paused and thought a moment. "But then again . . . I suppose most people cannot afford a library as extensive as mine. In any case, we really must be going. I am quite certain that we have already missed the first few numbers." With that, he popped the clip-on stud back into his mouth.

"If you hear anything about this burglary, give us a call on our cell phone," Sean said.

"Ob youd cadd con ob id," Spalding said.

"Sure," Sean replied. "Whatever."

The young detectives watched as Spalding and the others disappeared around the corner.

"Don't forget," Melissa shouted after them. "Call us!"

BRRRRRRRRP!

"Wow!" Sean said. "That was fast!" He pulled out the phone and answered, "Bloodhounds, Incorporated."

34

"I'm looking for the Hunter kids," said a shaky voice on the other end of the line.

"This is Sean Hunter."

"Well, this is Hildagard Tubbs."

"Hi, Mrs. Tubbs. What can we—"

"You kids had better get home right away," Mrs. Tubbs interrupted. "There are horrible noises coming out of your house."

"Noises?" Sean asked. "What kind of noises?"

"It sounds like someone's being . . . murdered!"

3

Jumpin' 'n' Jivin' Jeremiah

THURSDAY, 18:42 PDST

The kids were still a block away from home when they heard the horrible noise Mrs. Tubbs had spoken of.

EEROWWRROOOOEEE!

"What do you . . . *huff, puff* . . . think it is?" Melissa asked.

"I don't . . . *puff, huff* . . . know. But whatever it is, it's awful!"

Melissa agreed. It sounded like someone screaming over the whine of a table saw. "What if Dad's in there?" she cried.

Sean glanced at his watch. "Too early."

Melissa nodded. Their father rarely got home

from the radio station until late. But what if he
had decided to knock off early? What if he had
come home, and someone—or some*thing*—was
waiting for him in the house? The very thought
made her stomach flip-flop. She'd always loved
her father, but since their mother died of cancer
two years ago, now more than ever Melissa
couldn't bear the thought of something happening
to him. *Come on*, she scolded herself as her eyes
filled with tears, *it's just your imagination*.

She spotted Mrs. Tubbs in their front yard
with several neighbors. But they were all keeping
a safe distance from the house . . . and that
terrible noise.

"Has anyone gone in yet?" Sean shouted.

"Are you crazy?" Mrs. Tubbs cried. "I'm not
going in there."

"Me either!" another neighbor shouted.
"Whatever that is don't sound natural to me. I
think it's something from . . ." He paused for
effect, "from . . . beyond!"

"Oh, Harry," his wife scolded, "you're
watching too many of them *X-Files* reruns. You
think everything is from beyond."

"Do not."

"Do too. Remember last week? You thought the paper boy was from Jupiter."

"He was acting strange!" Harry argued.

"He was trying to collect what we owed him!" his wife said. "And when those Girl Scouts came to the door selling cookies, you begged them not to shoot you with their death rays!"

"It's not my fault they're making death rays look more and more like double chocolate mint boxes."

Meanwhile, Sean raced up to the front door, pulled it open, and ran inside. Melissa followed right behind.

"Wait!" Mrs. Tubbs shouted. "I've called the police! Let them handle—" But she was too late. The door . . .

*SLAMM*ed!

. . . shut.

After a moment, Harry's wife said, "Somebody ought to go in there and help them kids."

Another moment followed. (These neighbors weren't exactly a courageous bunch.)

Finally, summoning up all of her bravery and

courage, Mrs. Tubbs took a deep breath and spoke in her most heroic voice, "Oh, I'm sure they'll be just fine."

"Aren't they great?!" KC shouted over Spice Army's screaming guitars.

"Who's late?" Bear shouted back.

"No!" KC shook her head. "I said they're great! Really neat!"

"Something to eat?" Bear asked. "Whatcha got?"

"Never mind!" KC shouted.

"Melon rind?" Bear shouted back. "No thanks!"

KC turned to Spalding and started to say something, then stopped. Even if he could hear her, she couldn't understand him. Not with that big metal stud in his mouth. She sighed and sat back in her seat.

Up on stage, Spice Army was halfway through their new song, "C. Red Rooster Blues." Another strange title, but it didn't matter. As far as KC was concerned, the music was out of this world.

BEEP! BEEP! BOOP! WHRRRRRR!

In Doc's lab, the spectroscope jabbered away at lightning-fast speed. Doc stared at the flashing lights and rapidly wrote in her spiral notebook. It was only after she paused for a second that she noticed how violently her hands were shaking.

And for good reason!

The machine was supposed to be probing the deepest areas of outer space for signs of life—looking for messages that came from light-years away. But the signal on these messages was so strong that it couldn't possibly be coming from outer space. No, it was coming from some place much, much closer.

Questions raced through Doc's mind:

Are the aliens already on earth?

Are they ready to make their presence known?

And the biggest question of all . . .

Are they friendly?

Sean stopped as he entered their living room. With the blinds drawn, it was so dark that he couldn't see a thing. Neither could Melissa, who . . .

"OOOF!"

. . . banged into him from behind. Which caused Sean to let out a frightened . . .

"AHHHHH!"

Fortunately, the noise in the house was so loud that he couldn't be heard. And for that he was grateful. (Hey, a guy's got an image to keep, right?)

Melissa was the first to spot it. "Look!" she shouted.

Sean turned. There, on the family's big-screen television, with the volume cranked up as loud as it could go, was a glowing leprechaun-like creature. In his hands he held an electric guitar.

"Jeremiah!" Sean exclaimed.

For any of you newcomers, Jeremiah is made up completely of electrical energy. His name stands for *Johnson Electronic Reductive Entity Memory Inductive Assembly Housing.* He is one of Doc's first inventions and, as far as the kids were concerned, her best.

Now, he isn't exactly a real person (but don't try to tell him that). He's got all of the human traits: pride, selfishness, arrogance, impatience, stubbornness. . . . Hey, come to think of it, maybe he *is* a real person!

But whether or not that's true, one thing is for certain. In his early days he was involved with an unfortunate accident in a Chinese fortune-cookie company computer. It left his verbal memory chips somewhat scrambled. And to this day, Jeremiah's conversation is filled with proverbs and slogans that he never gets quite right.

Since he's made of electricity, he can go anywhere there's an electrical current. So he spends a lot of his time hanging out in Sean's digital watch or in the computer game Melissa keeps in her backpack. But today, unfortunately, he had chosen the family's brand-new big-screen TV.

However, now he looked a bit different. His hair was cut into a bright blue mohawk. His eyes were hidden behind sunglasses, and a lightning-bolt earring dangled from his left ear. Sparks flew from his fingers as they made their way up and down the guitar's strings. Although it was all very weird, it would have been okay . . . except for one little thing:

The music!

It was horrible! Imagine fifty pieces of chalk screeching on fifty different chalkboards at the same time, and you've got a pretty good idea of what we're talking about.

But Jeremiah didn't notice. He just kept strutting around with a look on his face that said, "Aren't I the greatest?!"

Sean grabbed the TV's volume control and turned it down as far as possible.

"Hey!" Jeremiah complained from the screen. "What did you do that for?"

"Because the neighbors are gathering in the yard," Melissa said.

"You mean they want my autograph already?" Jeremiah beamed. "Cool, and I haven't even released my first CD!"

"No, they don't want your autograph," Sean said.

"Oh." For the briefest moment Jeremiah looked depressed. But it would take more than that to deflate his ego. Suddenly he brightened. "Well, they may not want my autograph now, but they will. You know what they say, 'Build a better mousetrap and the world will beat you up.' "

" 'The world will beat a path to your door,' " Melissa corrected.

"Whatever." Jeremiah shrugged. "Anyway, I've been practicing my guitar because I'm going to start a brand-new band."

"Yeah?"

"Yeah. We're calling ourselves . . . OutaSync."

"OutaSync?" Sean asked.

"That's right." Jeremiah grinned.

"Well, judging by your music," Melissa said, "I'd guess that's a pretty good name."

"Thank you." Jeremiah's face changed from green to red (which is an electronic character's version of blushing).

"I didn't know you were interested in music," Sean said.

"I wasn't," Jeremiah answered, "until last night. That's when I heard the Spice Army concert, and—"

"Concert?" Melissa asked. "How did you hear the concert?"

"On your dad's station," Jeremiah replied. "He's carrying them live all week, remember? Anyway, as soon as I heard them, I knew I was born to boogie."

"You weren't exactly born," Melissa reminded him.

"Okay, then I was manufactured for makin' music."

Melissa rolled her eyes.

"Well, listen, ol' buddy," Sean said. "Whatever you were makin', it isn't exactly mus—"

"Gotta go!"

Before Sean could even finish his sentence, Jeremiah had disappeared, leaving the TV screen dark. That's when the young detectives first noticed the approaching siren.

"The police!" Melissa exclaimed. "Mrs. Tubbs said she called the police! What are we going to tell them about the noise?"

"I have no idea," Sean said. "We certainly can't tell them the truth!"

"But we can't lie!" Melissa argued. "You know how God feels about lying."

"I know! I know!" Sean said. Man, it was hard to be a Christian sometimes—especially in the detective business where truth-telling can get you into trouble, especially if—

SCREEEETCH!

Car brakes squealed in front of the house. Melissa peeked out the window. "You'd better come up with something fast!" she said. "They're here!"

"I'll tell 'em you make a terrible noise when you sing!" Sean shouted.

"Sean!"

"Well, it's true. You do!"

"How could I have been in here singing when everybody saw me out there?"

"Oh yeah."

The police car's doors opened and two patrolmen got out—a short, fat guy and a tall, skinny one. Both were trying their best to look important and official.

"They seem awfully young," Sean said. "They must be right out of the police academy."

Suddenly their patrol car started rolling backward down the street. Unfortunately, both officers were too busy looking official to notice.

"Your car!" Harry, the neighbor, shouted.

"You forgot to set your emergency brake!"

The tall officer turned to see their car picking up speed as it headed down the street. "Phil!" he shouted. "Someone's trying to steal our car!"

"What?" The short, fat one spun around, then shouted, "Stop in the name of the law!" He reached for his gun but couldn't get it out of the holster, so he started running after the car. "Stop! I order you to stop! Stop right now!" All of this as he kept trying to pull out his gun. "In the name of the law, I order you to—

"WHOOPS!"

Apparently, he'd been pulling on the wrong belt. Which would explain why his pants suddenly fell to the ground . . . revealing a lovely pair of boxer shorts, covered with cute little teddy bears.

But that wasn't the end of his little adventure. The fallen pants made him . . .

WHUMP!

. . . trip, falling face first to the ground. Unfortunately, this also knocked his handgun out of its holster.

The crowd gasped as the pistol flew, twisting

and turning, high into the air.

They gasped again as it came down and
landed hard on the . . .

KER-KLUNK!

. . . street, and . . .

KA-POWIE!

. . . fired!

KA-POWIE!

Twice!

The neighbors scattered in all directions. They
wanted to get out of there before the Midvale
Police Department turned them into Swiss cheese!

"Don't worry, folks!" the tall one shouted.
"They don't let us use real bullets, do they, Phil!"

"That's right, Bill," the shorter one cried.
"They're only pellets."

Pellets shmellets. Whatever was coming out of
those guns, it was still dangerous as . . .

ZZZZINGGGGG . . .

. . . the first pellet passed so close to Mrs. Tubbs'
nose that it made her . . .

"AH-CHOO!"

. . . sneeze. Then it . . .

PFFFTTT . . .

. . . knocked the lighted tip off Harry's cigarette. (Which was very good because he'd been trying to quit smoking for years.) And finally it . . .

KA-THWACK!

. . . lodged into the side of Mrs. Tubbs' house.

Meanwhile, pellet number two's journey was equally as interesting as it . . .

KA-CHUNK!

. . . splintered the cute little wooden bluebirds that decorated someone's mailbox. Then . . .

KA-ZING!

. . . ricocheted off the fire hydrant on the corner. And . . .

KA-POW! SHHhhhh . . .

. . . blew out the tire of the runaway patrol car, causing it to veer to the left, smash into an ancient oak tree, and finally, mercifully, come to rest. But the hornets' nest, directly above it, did not rest. It swayed first to the left, then to the right, then to the left again.

All this as the officers ran to the car, Phil hiking up his pants along the way. Still under the impression that someone had tried to steal his car, he arrived, grabbed the driver's side door, yanked it open, and shouted, "Get out of the car with your hands up!"

Unfortunately, this was just enough extra movement to make the hornets' nest . . .

(You're way ahead of me here, aren't you?)

. . . fall from the tree and . . .

KER-PLUNK!

. . . land directly on Officer Phil's head!

"Get it off!" he shouted. "Get it off!" He ran in circles, holding his pants up with one hand, trying to pull off the nest with the other.

Patrolman Bill ran right behind. "Slow down!" he shouted. "You're moving too fast! Slow down!"

But instead of slowing down, Phil picked up speed. Wearing the hornets' nest like a turban, he took off for who knows where, with Bill in hot pursuit.

Sean and Melissa watched all of this from their living room window in utter amazement. Who were those guys? But before either could speak—

BEEP! BEEP! BEEP!

—Sean's digital watch went off.

"What is it?" Melissa asked.

Pushing up his sleeve for a better look, Sean said, "It's an email from Doc."

"And. . . ?"

"She says she's getting a message from . . . oh, you're not going to like this."

"Tell me," Melissa insisted.

"You're not going to like this one bit."

"Sean . . ."

"She says she's getting a message from . . . outer space."

4

"Collect Call From Mars . . . Will You Accept the Charges?"

THURSDAY, 19:11 PDST

The kids headed for Doc's house as fast as they could—Sean on his skateboard, being pulled along by Slobs, and Melissa on her Silver Scooter.

About a block away from Doc's house, Slobs suddenly came to a screeching stop.

Sean was not so lucky!

His skateboard shot off in one direction. He shot off . . .

"Yiiiiii! Look out!"

. . . in the other. In fact, he flew through the air

like a guy shot out of a cannon at the circus. Only, for him, there was no safety net! There was only . . .

"OOOOOOMPH!"

. . . the flower bed, which he landed in face first. But instead of racing to help him, Slobs remained stationary. She tilted her head back and forth as if listening to something very painful, and then she let out a big . . .

"AROOOOOOO!"

. . . howl. Without a moment's hesitation, she turned and ran home.

Meanwhile, Sean was . . .

"SPPFFTT! THFRTT!"

. . . spitting up petunias. When he finally got enough out of his mouth to speak, he turned to Melissa and asked, "What's the matter with Slobs?"

"Got me," Melissa answered. "She acts like she's hearing something. And whatever it is, she doesn't like it!"

When the kids finally made it to Doc's house, they found that she was still bent over her spectroscope, which was clicking, beeping, and whirring away.

Sean grabbed hold of a long stream of computer paper that was spitting from the machine. "This make any sense to you?" he asked, shoving it to his sister.

Melissa looked at it and shook her head. The paper was covered with strange-looking symbols: ovals, triangles, and zigzags going off in different directions.

Suddenly all the clicking and beeping stopped. The spectroscope hiccuped once and then . . .

All was still.

The three of them stood in silence, staring at the machine, expecting it to start up again. When it didn't, Sean picked up the computer paper and showed it to Doc.

What is this? he signed.

Doc stepped to her keyboard and typed her answer. *This is a message from* . . . she nodded toward the ceiling . . . *out there.*

"Wow!" Sean whispered. "Now what?"

Now I've got to translate it. And that could

take hours. Maybe days. I'll also have to see if I can pinpoint its origin.

"Where do you think it's coming from?" Melissa asked.

Doc shrugged, then did her best to avoid their eyes.

"Doc?" Melissa tapped her on the shoulder. But still, the woman wouldn't look at her. "Doc?"

Finally Doc reached back to the keyboard and typed, *It could be from anywhere. Now don't bother me. I have work to do.*

Melissa and Sean exchanged glances. Something was definitely up. And whatever it was, Doc was keeping it from them.

THURSDAY, 23:00 PDST

"Sis? You asleep?"

"No, come on in."

Melissa lay in bed, making doodles in a notebook. Slobs lay curled on the floor beside her, sound asleep, happily chasing cats or rabbits or doggie biscuits.

Sean plunked himself down on the edge of her bed. "Can't sleep," he said.

"Me either."

"I'm still trying to figure out what Doc was hiding from us." Sean shook his head. "That's not like her."

"I know." Melissa sighed and put down her notebook.

Sean picked it up. "What are you doing? This looks weird."

"It's just some anagrams," she answered.

"Some ana-whats?"

"Anagrams. I read a magazine article about them. It's kind of interesting."

"What are they?"

"You just take the letters in somebody's name or in a book title or something, and move them around to see what else they might spell."

Sean frowned. "I'm not following you."

"Well, take 'Sean Hunter,' " she said as she retrieved her notebook and wrote his name. "We move the letters around and it becomes 'here's an nut.' "

"That's stupid," Sean grumped. "Nobody says, 'Here's *an* nut.' It's 'here's *a* nut.' "

She shrugged. "Sometimes it doesn't work out perfectly."

He grabbed the notebook. "Let me try."

" 'Melissa Hunter,' " he said. "Let's see . . . 'she's a runt. . . . ' "

"Sean . . ."

BRRRP! BRRRP!

"Who could be calling us at this hour?" Melissa asked.

"Only one way to find out." Sean flipped open the phone and answered, "Bloodhounds, Incorporated."

"This is Mr. Petersen, from the bookstore."

"Hello, Mr. Petersen."

"I'm sorry to be calling so late, but I just came across an important clue, and I thought you'd want to know about it."

"What's that?" Sean asked.

"Someone brought back one of the books that was stolen," he said. "Apparently the thief dropped it in an alley."

"Go on."

"Well, there's something stuck on it—a little round tie clip or something. And it's got an initial on it."

"An initial?" Sean asked.

"Yes," Mr. Petersen replied. "An *S*. Anyway, maybe you can check it for fingerprints. I'm pretty sure if you find out who dropped this, you'll find your thief."

5

Spalding, How Could You?

FRIDAY, 11:14 PDST

"Sean, we both know who this belongs to," Melissa said as she held up the little silver stud they'd retrieved from the bookstore.

"No, we don't," Sean said. "Not for sure."

"It's got a big white *S* on it," Melissa said. "Who else could it possibly belong to?"

"I'll bet lots of people have clip-on studs for their tongues with the letter *S* on them," he argued.

"Yeah, like who?"

"Uh . . . Sylvester Stallone?"

"Right," Melissa said. "Like Sylvester Stallone came to Midvale, broke into the bookstore, and stole a bunch of weird textbooks."

"It could happen," Sean said.

"Oh, come on! This thing belongs to Spalding and you know it! And if you ask me, he's carrying this tough-guy, rock 'n' roll image way too far."

"Yeah," Sean sighed. "I guess you're right. I just hate to think that Spalding . . ."

"Me too! So what should we do? I personally think—"

GRRRRRRRRR!

"What's that?" Melissa gasped. "A bear?"

"Sorry." Sean pointed at his stomach. "It was me."

Melissa gave him one of her famous death looks, and he shrugged. Finally she sighed and said, "Well, it is almost lunchtime. So . . . you got any money?"

"Me? Are you kidding? How about you?"

Melissa shook her head. "Not enough for lunch."

"Well, then, I guess we swing by the radio station and see if Dad wants to take us out," Sean said.

Melissa smiled her sweetest smile and asked, "How could he resist?"

FRIDAY, 11:47 PDST

"Hi, guys! What's up?" Dad was obviously in a good mood. "Glad you came by. You want to grab a bite to eat?"

GRRRRRRRRRRR!

"Yeah, I guess you do," he laughed.

"I didn't have much for breakfast," Sean said.

"You had three waffles, two pancakes, five pieces of bacon, and six sausages!" Melissa exclaimed.

"Yeah," Sean agreed. "Like I said, not much."

Dad laughed. "Let me take care of some paper work, and we'll be on our way."

"Sure," Melissa said. "Take your time."

Dad hummed to himself as he started arranging the papers on his desk.

"You seem to be really up today," Sean said.

"I am," Dad answered. "Did you know that KRZY has been broadcasting the Spice Army concerts?"

"Yeah," the kids said.

"Well, they've just asked us to work with other stations around the state and do a simulcast. And sponsors are coming out of the woodwork wanting to pay for advertising time."

"Cool," Sean said. "Does that mean KRZY won't be in debt up to its eyeballs anymore?"

"That's right." Dad grinned. "After today's concert, we'll just be up to our kneecaps."

"That's great!" Melissa exclaimed. "Is that why Herbie's in the other room working on the transmitter? We saw him as we were coming in."

"Right," Dad said. "They wanted to make sure we were utilizing all of our power. This is going to be a big day for KRZY! In fact, we might even—"

KA-BLOOM!

The lights flickered and the ground shook.

"What was that!" Melissa cried.

"A sonic boom?" Sean shouted.

"I don't think so," Dad said.

"An earthquake?" Melissa asked.

"I'm afraid not."

"Then it has to be . . ."

All three turned toward the engineer's room

and cried in perfect unison:

"Herbie!"

Poor Herbie. If there was an accident to be had, the klutz-extraordinaire station engineer would have it. And by the look of things, he'd just found himself a doozy.

"Herbie!" Dad called. "Are you okay?"

"Sure, sure. Fine, fine." He might have been a bit more convincing if smoke weren't rising from his clothes as he staggered into the room. Then, of course, there was his hair that stood on end, not to mention a face that was completely covered in soot.

"I'm fine," he repeated. "Just a little explosion. I've been in worse." He coughed twice, emitting two little black clouds of smoke. Then, shaking his head, he mumbled, "Maybe that green wire was supposed to connect to the blue one instead of the red."

"You sure you don't need a doctor?" Dad asked.

"Nah. I'm fine." Herbie gave a weak smile that showed he wasn't all that fine.

"You sure?"

"Fine, fine."

"What about the equipment?"

"Oh, it's fine." Herbie sounded even less convincing.

"Well, listen," Dad said, "the kids and I were just about to grab some lunch. You want to come with us?"

"You bet. Just give me a minute to clean up."

After Herbie went into the rest room, Dad asked, "You guys don't mind, do you? He's had kind of a rough day."

"No, we don't mind," Melissa answered. But the words had barely left her lips before, suddenly, they heard:

"Help me! Help me!"

"It's coming from the rest room!" Dad said. Immediately he was on his feet, rushing toward the door. "Herbie, what's wrong? Are you all right?"

"It's my hands!" came the panicked cry. "They're stuck to the hand dryer!"

Another fifteen minutes passed before Herbie

was free and everyone was safely in Dad's car heading to lunch.

"That was really weird," Dad said. "How did you get stuck to the dryer like that?"

"Beats me." Herbie shook his head.

"I thought we'd never get you unstuck," Sean said.

"Hey, Dad, can we try this place?" Melissa pointed out the window at Midvale's newest restaurant, *The Ravishing Radish*.

"Sure," Dad answered. "Sounds great. And look, there's a parking place right in front!" He eased the car into the parking spot and everyone jumped out.

Everyone except Herbie, that is.

"What's wrong, Herbie?" Melissa asked.

"I can't seem to let go of the door handle!"

"Are you sure you don't need to see a doctor?" Dad asked when they had finally pried him loose.

"No, I'm . . . fine. Honest. Here, let me put a couple of quarters in the parking meter." He fished in his pocket for coins as he walked up to the meter. And then . . .

KER-WHAP!

. . . Herbie was suddenly hugging that parking meter as if his life depended on it. His arms and legs were wrapped around the pole, and his cheek was pressed against the little window on the meter.

"Herbie!" Sean cried. "What in the world are you trying to—"

"Look!" Melissa pointed at the arrow in the window that tells how much time is left. It was swinging wildly back and forth.

Two hours . . . five minutes . . . forty-five minutes . . . twenty minutes . . .

Dad ran to Herbie's side to help. "Come on, guys! Help me get him loose!" But as he approached, his expensive fountain pen came flying out of his shirt pocket and . . .

THUNK!

. . . stuck tight to the side of Herbie's head.

Next came the empty can that was lying in the gutter.

K-THWACK

"Ow!" Herbie cried. But before he could say anything more, two members of the Midvale

Garden Club passed by, looking down their noses at him.

"Well, I never!" the first woman said. "He's so drunk he can't even stand up!"

"Why, he's just disgusting," the other woman agreed.

But no sooner were the words out of her mouth than she flew in Herbie's direction, wrapping her arms around him.

"Blanche!" the other woman demanded. "What are you doing!"

"It's not me!" Blanche cried. "It's this brooch!" She pointed at the heavy metal pendant on her sweater. "It pulled me to him!"

"A likely story!" the other woman sniffed, then turned and headed down the street alone.

Melissa snapped her fingers. "He's been magnetized!"

"I'll bet it's from the explosion," Sean agreed. "He's become an electromagnet. That explains the hand dryer."

"What's going to happen to me?" Herbie whined.

"Don't worry," Sean assured him. "It shouldn't last too long." Then he added under his breath, "No more than a day or two."

It wasn't easy, but they managed to pry
Blanche away from Herbie, then Herbie away
from the parking meter . . . until finally they
made their way into the restaurant and took their
seats in a booth.

Once they got settled, Melissa turned to her
father. "Dad," she said, "we need some advice."

"You've come to the right place," Dad said.
"If I don't know, Herbie will. Right, Herb?"

Herbie smiled but didn't say anything. He was
too busy looking around making sure heavy
metal objects weren't flying in his direction.

"Well, if you have a friend who's kind of
starting to dress like a . . . a . . ."

"Thug," Sean finished her sentence.

"Yeah, a thug . . . you know, somebody real
dark and shady . . . should you talk to him? I
mean, what if he's not really a bad guy but just
wants to look like one?"

Nobody but Herbie noticed the silverware on
the table starting to vibrate.

Dad nodded. "I think I understand. He just wants to look cool."

"Right," Melissa said. "Well, is that okay, or should we talk to him?"

Herbie stared, frightened, as knives, forks, and spoons slowly started moving across the table in his direction.

Not noticing them, Dad answered Melissa. "Well, I don't think you can judge anyone because of the way he looks. But the Bible says that God expects us to avoid even the appearance of evil. So if your friend is starting to dress like someone bad, then he's already doing something wrong. I think you need to talk to him before other people start misjudging him."

"But he's a pretty good guy," Sean said.

"I understand." Dad nodded. "But Jesus said we're supposed to let our light shine so others can see God's love in us. You can't let your light shine if you run around looking like a criminal. That's really the bottom li—"

"Ahhh . . ."

CLANK! CLINK! CLUNK!

The silverware picked up speed, banging into

each other as they crawled across the table, until . . .

THWACK!

. . . a spoon jumped up to Herbie's nose. Next . . .

THUNK!

. . . a fork stuck to his chin (prongs first, of course).

"YEOW!"

And before you knew it . . .

KA-CHINK! KA-CHUNK! KA-CHANK!

. . . Herbie's face was covered with silverware. Unfortunately, that wasn't the end of his little mishap.

"Look out!" Sean shouted.

Now silverware from other tables flew across the room. One man was preparing to take a bite of his chicken fried steak when . . .

WHISK

. . . his fork flew out of his hand.

The waitress was pouring coffee when the pot . . .

WHOOSH

. . . flew out of her hands. And then suddenly . . .

BANG! POW! CLANK!

What in the world? Everyone's eyes turned toward the kitchen. The kitchen door swung open and . . .

Uh-oh!

. . . a collection of pots, pans, and utensils were flying straight for Herbie.

"YEEOWWW!"

He jumped up from the table and ran for the door. The pots and pans followed right behind, gaining on him. He made it outside just ahead of them and ran up the street, passing a couple of punkers with nose rings and other piercings.

"Whoa, dude!" one of them yelled when he saw all the silverware stuck to Herbie's face. "Where'd you get all the cool stuff?"

"Man!" the other said, equally as impressed. "That's one baaad dude!"

Meanwhile, back in the restaurant, Dad plunked down a twenty-dollar bill. "You guys go ahead and order," he said. "I'll go see if I can help Herbie." But he'd barely left the table before . . .

BEEP! BEEP! BEEP!

"Good grief!" Sean whined. "It looks like we'll never get to eat." (Eating is an important thing to Sean, if you hadn't noticed.) With a heavy sigh, he pulled back his sleeve and looked at his digital watch. "It's another email from Doc," he said. "She's almost finished her translation of the message from space." Then he frowned.

"What's up?" Melissa asked.

"I don't know," he said, continuing to read the message. "But why would aliens be interested in Midvale State Bank?"

6

We Come in Peace, Now Stick 'Em Up!

"Tell me what it says," Melissa demanded. "Tell me what Doc's email says."

Sean reached out his arm with the watch for her to see. "Here. Read it yourself."

Melissa stared at it and frowned. "Very funny," she said. "Now where's the message from Doc?"

"Whadd'ya mean, it's right here." Sean pulled the watch back. "It says . . . whoa, what is this?"

Where Doc's message had once been, there was now a strange jumble of characters and symbols.

"Let's go," Sean said. "This looks serious."

FRIDAY, 13:21 PDST

Doc nodded as Sean showed her the jumble of figures that had once been her email. She strode across the room, picked up a piece of paper that sat on the spectroscope's keyboard, and handed it to him.

"What is this?" he asked.

Doc signed, *It's part of the message I got this morning*.

"This is just like the writing on your watch!" Melissa exclaimed.

"It sure is," Sean said. "But what does it mean?"

Melissa turned to Doc. "Have you translated it yet?"

Doc shook her head and signed, *Not this one. But here's the one I got yesterday*. She picked up another piece of paper and handed it to Melissa, who cleared her throat and began to read,

"Midvale State Bank. Something something target. Best time to strike something is Saturday something something. . . ."

"It sounds like they're planning some sort of invasion!" Sean shouted.

"Or a bank robbery!" Melissa exclaimed.

Sean stepped to the computer keyboard and typed, *Did you ever figure out where this message came from?*

Doc nodded and typed, *That's the weirdest thing. I didn't want to tell you this before, but it seems to be coming from KRZY radio.*

"Dad's station!" Sean exclaimed.

I know, Doc typed. *That's why I didn't want to tell you before. I wanted to make sure.*

Melissa stepped up to the keyboard and typed, *But I thought these messages were supposed to be from outer space!*

Doc nodded. *Based on the angle of the signals, I don't think they're originating directly from the station. It's more like the station is amplifying and broadcasting an existing signal coming from somewhere else that—*

BRRRRRP! BRRRRP!

Sean reached for his phone. "Hello . . . er . . . I mean, Bloodhounds, Incorporated." He looked at his watch. "You're right. I'm sorry. Yes, ma'am, we'll be right there."

"Who was it?" Melissa asked.

"Mrs. Welton, from the drugstore. Remember, it was burglarized the same night as the bookstore."

"Oh, that's right, we promised her we'd be there—"

"Fifteen minutes ago," Sean said. Then, looking at his watch, he frowned. "I don't understand it. I know I set this alarm to remind me."

Doc, who had to be the world's best lip-reader, stepped to her keyboard and typed, *I'll bet they turned it off.*

"They?" Sean asked. "What do you mean *they?*"

Whoever's been sending these messages. Sometimes when a message is coming in, alarms go off that aren't set. But then this morning my alarm didn't *go off.*

Sean and Melissa exchanged puzzled looks.

And that's not all, Doc continued. *I always lock my doors when I go to bed at night, and this morning they were all unlocked.*

"Are they doing this on purpose?" Sean asked.

I don't know. I think it has something to do with the super high-pitched frequency they're using.

"High-pitched?" Sean asked.

"You mean like only a dog could hear?" Melissa asked.

That's right, Doc signed.

Melissa nodded. "Which would explain why Slobs has been acting so weird . . ."

Mrs. Welton shook her head. "They made an absolute mess in this store."

Sean looked around at the jumble of merchandise. Card racks overturned . . . scarves twisted on the floor . . . costume jewelry hanging in and out of drawers. "They sure did," he agreed.

"Oh, not here," Mrs. Welton said. "Our customers did all this. We're having a clearance sale. I mean over there!" She ushered them into another area of the store. "See what a terrible mess it is?"

Sean and Melissa exchanged glances. The

section looked 100% neater than the rest of the store.

"So what did they get?" Sean asked.

"They?"

"You know, the burglars."

"Oh . . . well, they didn't really take anything."

Melissa frowned. "Then what did they—"

"Rearranged all the merchandise in here, that's what they did," Mrs. Welton replied. "It's going to take weeks for us to get it back the way it was before."

"I see," Sean said, even though he didn't see at all. As far as he was concerned, the burglars should have left a bill for cleaning. "And do you have any idea why someone would want to break in here and . . . uh . . . mess things up like this?"

Mrs. Welton shook her head. "Just to see if they could get away with it, I suppose." She sighed as if she were heartbroken by the mess in front of her. "Well, I'll leave you two alone so you can look for clues."

After she had left, Melissa turned to her brother. "So what do we do?" she asked.

He shrugged. "The usual, I guess. Dust for

fingerprints. That kind of thing."

"Okay, I'll—OW!"

"What happened?" Sean asked.

"I stepped on something . . . a marble, I think." She bent down and picked it up off the floor. As she held it up, they both gasped.

It was a little silver stud with a clip on one end . . . and a big white *S* on the other.

Sean shook his head. "We'd better go talk to that boy and talk to him *now*!"

FRIDAY, 15:15 PDST

Spalding was already sitting beneath the big oak tree in the park when Sean and Melissa got there. As he promised, he was alone. Just him and his baggy pants, ripped T-shirt, giant pocket chain, and tattoos.

"So, what is it you wished to converse with me about?" he asked. "Am I a suspect in one of your cases?" He chuckled, but it was a nervous chuckle.

Sean held up one of the tongue studs. "Does this belong to you?"

"Why, yes, thank you. Where did you find it?" He took the tongue stud out of Sean's hand, wiped it off with his shirt, and popped it back into his mouth.

"At the bookstore . . . the one that was broken into."

Spalding's face turned the slightest bit pink, and he took the stud back out of his mouth. "What are you implying? I go to the bookstore quite frequently. It simply fell out of my pocket, that's all."

Melissa held up the other stud.

"And what about this one?" she asked.

"Where'd you find. . . ?"

"At the drugstore," Melissa answered. "It was robbed, too."

Spalding sputtered, "Well, that looks like mine, but I . . ."

"Where'd you get these things, anyway?" Melissa asked.

"I had them manufactured," Spalding said.

"Where?" Sean asked.

"One of the roadies offered to produce them for me."

"Roadie?" Melissa repeated. "What's a roadie?"

"A fellow who travels with the band," Spalding explained. "He sets up their sound system and such. Listen," he insisted, "I have done nothing wrong. You must believe me!"

"If that's true," Melissa said, "then maybe you ought to stop dressing like a . . . a . . . whatever it is you're supposed to be."

"There is nothing at all wrong with my attire!" Spalding snapped.

"But, Spalding," Melissa said, "if you dress the part, people are bound to think that—"

"Don't preach to me," Spalding snapped. "I like my appearance, and I will continue to dress as such!"

"Listen," Sean said, "Mr. Petersen over at the bookstore told us if we found the person that stud belonged to, we'd find our crook. Mrs. Welton at the drugstore feels the same way."

"Well, I don't care how they feel," Spalding said. "I have done nothing illegal, and that is that. Now, if you don't mind, I shall be leaving."

He clipped the stud back on his tongue—a bit too tight, as it happened, which made his nose tickle . . . which made him . . .

"Ahh . . . Ahh . . . Ahh . . ."

. . . have to . . .

"AH-CHOO!"

When he sneezed, the little stud of silver flew out of his mouth at about 98.3 miles per hour. It shot across the street until . . .

K-RASH!

. . . it smashed through the windshield of a passing police car. The car hit its . . .

SCREETCH!

. . . brakes, skidded to a stop, and both doors flew open to reveal . . .

"Oh no!" Melissa moaned. "It's Phil and Bill!"

Sure enough, the two officers thought someone was shooting at them. They already had their pellet guns drawn and were ready to return fire.

"Run, Spalding!" Sean shouted. "Run!"

And run he did!

7

Message in the Music

Fortunately for Spalding, the two police officers were about five seconds too late to notice him taking off. Instead, they stood back to back, with pellet guns drawn, turning in a circle, scanning the neighborhood.

When he was sure all was safe, Phil returned his gun to its holster and went over to check out their windshield. Bill, his partner, joined him.

"Well, I'll be, Phil. What you suppose it is?"

"Got me, Bill. But whatever it is, it's got a big *S* on it."

Sean and Melissa winced as Officer Bill scratched his head with the barrel of his gun. "Hey, Phil," he said, "you know what this is, don't you?"

"What's that, Bill?"

"It's a clue, Phil!"

"A clue?" Phil repeated the word as if it were something mysterious and special. "Wow! I've never seen a clue before."

"So what do we do with it now, Phil?"

"Guess we take it back to the station, Bill. Maybe the chief'll know what we ought to do with—"

K-BLAMMM!

A nearby truck picked an unfortunate time to backfire. Immediately, the officers took aim with their guns and this time began . . .

POW! POW! POW!

. . . firing back at just about everything that moved, and a few things that didn't. Shoppers scrambled for cover as pellets whizzed over their heads.

BLAM!

There went the streetlight on the corner of Ramsey and Main. That'll show that light!

KA-POW!

That nasty old stop sign took one in the shoulder.

POW! POW! POW!

And the sign that read, *Shop Midvale, the Friendliest Town in the USA*, took a dozen blasts.

Fortunately for the good citizens of Midvale, the two policemen eventually ran out of pellets.

Doubly fortunately, they hadn't hurt anyone . . . well, except for the six windows, five car headlights, four signs, two streetlights, and one inflatable gorilla some mom was taking home to her kid.

Officer Bill looked around at the damage and smiled. "Midvale's safe now, Phil. Everything's nice and quiet."

And he was right. The streets that had been crowded with shoppers were now empty. Even the park was deserted. The only sound was the squeaking swing that swung back and forth in the afternoon breeze.

Bill thrust his revolver back into its holster.

POW!

"Ow! My foot! My foot!"

What do you know . . . I guess he had one pellet left.

FRIDAY, 18:20 PDST

Finally! At last! Melissa couldn't believe that she and her brother were really going to get to hear Spice Army in person!

She looked around the crowded amphitheater. Among the many "normal-looking" people, there were dozens of kids covered with tattoos and body piercings, young people totally devoted to Spice Army.

"Ladies and gentlemen!" the announcer's voice boomed. "Please give a hearty welcome to the one, the only . . . SPICE ARMY!"

A roar went up from the crowd, which was immediately drowned out by blasting . . .

SCREEEEEE-OOOOOOO-EEEEEEEE!

. . . guitars and . . .

THWACKA-BOOM-BOOM-BOOM-TWHACKA!

. . . drums.

As they played, Melissa wondered if maybe Spice Army sounded a little better on CD than they did in person. And, by the way, what in the world was that instrument with the keyboard? It looked an awful lot like . . . Doc's spectrograph.

But before she had a chance to give it another thought, the volume of the music suddenly . . .

K-RRRACCCCKed!

. . . Sean's digital watch, unleashing Jeremiah as . . .

OUTASYNC!

That's right, there he was on stage, in all his green glory, making that same horrible noise with his guitar that he'd made yesterday afternoon in Sean and Melissa's living room.

And the audience loved it!

In fact, the guys from Spice Army even stood back to let him play a moment. Melissa couldn't believe it. Nobody screamed. Nobody ran. As best she figured, this was the first time that a public appearance by Jeremiah hadn't touched off a panic.

He strutted back and forth on stage, giving a loud, ear-piercing shriek from his electrical guitar. When he finished, the crowd jumped to its feet and gave a tremendous ovation—screaming, whistling, clapping, and stomping their approval.

"Thank you!" he shouted. "I'm OutaSync and I love you! Let me leave you with one important word of wisdom. If at first you don't succeed . . . please don't take up skydiving! Good night!"

There was a brilliant flash, and then he was gone.

Spice Army's lead singer stepped back to his microphone and shouted, "I don't know who that dude was, but he was great! And now, here's a special song for all of our friends in the Spice Army army . . . 'Oil-Browned Bully'!"

Man! Melissa thought. *They sure have some weird song titles.* She pulled a pen and a scrap of paper from her purse and wrote down the title "Oil-Browned Bully." A moment later she started moving the letters around.

Sean looked at her and smiled. "Still on an anagram kick?" he shouted.

Melissa nodded and continued writing until, suddenly, "Uhh!" She sucked in her breath. Then she held up the paper to Sean.

He stared at it a moment, his eyes widening. When rearranged, the letters from "Oil-Browned Bully" spelled out, "We'll rob you blind!"

8

Spalding Hits a Sour Note

FRIDAY, 21:42 PDST

"I'm telling you, it's just a coincidence!" Sean insisted. He stood at the stove, fixing himself and his sister some hot chocolate after the concert.

"Coincidence?" Melissa shook her head. "Think about it for a minute. All the burglaries Thursday night took place during the time Spice Army was on stage at the amphitheater."

"So. . . ?" Sean shrugged and continued to stir the pan of hot chocolate.

"So then tonight they play a song that translates into " 'We'll rob you blind.' "

"So. . . ?"

"So listen to these three songs they played right after that first one:

" 'Dream on, Pretty Stace,' which, when I rearrange the letters, spells out 'Ace Department Story.' Obviously it's Ace Department Store."

Sean turned to her, still not convinced, but getting interested. "Go on."

"The next one was 'Devil Man Ride,' which is pretty weird all by itself. But when you translate it, it spells, 'Midvale Diner.' "

"Okay."

"And finally, there was 'Clearly Lee's Tonic,' which becomes 'Electronics Alley.' "

By now Melissa definitely had Sean's attention. She continued, "Each of these places is a store in Midvale, right?"

"Yeah?"

"Well, if each of these stores was broken into during the concert last night, we'll know there's a connection."

"You just might be on to something," Sean admitted.

"And you know that big hit 'Artful Moosey'?"

"Yeah?"

"That translates into 'steal from you.' "

Sean nodded in thought. "Maybe you're right;

maybe they *are* sending signals to somebody. But what about Spalding?"

"I don't know." Melissa frowned. "Maybe they've brainwashed him or something. Or maybe they're just using him in some way."

Sean snapped his fingers. "I just thought of something!"

"Wow! Did it hurt?"

"No." Sean glared. "Listen. Remember Doc said that ever since she's been picking up those messages from space, her doors have been locking and unlocking, and alarms have been turning on and off."

Melissa's face brightened. "You're right! What if they could unlock those stores' locks by sending out some kind of signal!"

"And what if they can also turn off their alarms?" Sean asked.

"And if they could do it with the stores . . . remember that message about Midvale Bank?"

"You're right!" Sean said. "If they could do it with the stores, they'll be able to do it with the bank!"

"And since nothing was stolen from the stores . . ."

"They were just practicing, getting ready for the real thing!"

"All right," Melissa said. "First thing in the morning, we'll go to Doc's and ask her if she's picked up any more messages. Oh, and Sean?"

"Huh?"

"Your hot chocolate is on fire!"

She wasn't kidding! The milk had boiled completely out of the pan, and long fingers of flames shot out of whatever was left.

"YIIII . . ." He yanked it off the burner and ran for the back door. "Outta my way! Outta my way!"

SATURDAY, 9:41 PDST

When they arrived at Doc's, the young detectives were disappointed to find the spectrograph sitting still and silent. Doc sat at her desk, bent over the earlier messages, still trying to translate them.

The TV in the corner was tuned to *Saturday Morning News* with Midvale's intrepid reporter,

Rafael Ruelas. Ruelas was very excited about something. You could tell by the way he was waving his arms and jumping up and down.

"He's really wound up today," Sean noted.

Melissa rolled her eyes. "He's always wound up about something."

"I wonder what he's talking about?"

"Why don't you turn up the volume and find out?" Melissa asked.

"Oh yeah." Sean stepped to the television and did as his sister suggested.

Honestly, Melissa wondered, *do I have to think of everything?*

Suddenly Ruelas's voice was rattling away. "Nobody knows where he came from, but this new talent, who calls himself OutaSync, is the best this reporter has seen in a long, long time."

The camera pulled back for a wider view. Ruelas was surrounded by teenagers who were pushing one another out of the way so they could be seen. Several had painted themselves green to look like OutaSync.

"So"—Ruelas thrust his microphone at one particularly goofy-looking boy—"what do you think of OutaSync?"

"He's totally cool, man."

"OutaSync rules, wahooooo!" somebody shouted.

"Green powerrrrr!" another yelled.

The camera zoomed in to a tight shot of Ruelas as the OutaSync fans kept trying to get in the picture. "In other news," Ruelas said, "Midvale police report that they are very close to ridding the city of a daring gang of criminal masterminds known only as 'S.' Just last night several Midvale businesses were broken into during the Spice Army concert."

Sean hit the channel selector. "Hey, sis, you know what channel *Scooby Doo* is on?"

"Sean . . ."

"What?"

"He was just about to say what stores were robbed last night!"

"So. . . ?"

"So that was the info we were waiting for."

"Come on, sis. We're talking about Scooby, Scrappy, and friends, here. We can find out that other stuff—"

Suddenly Melissa jumped up. "I got it!" she cried.

"Got what?"

She motioned for Doc to give her a pencil and a piece of paper. "Look what happens when you rearrange the letters in Spice Army."

She shoved the paper at her brother.

"Crime pays!" he gasped. " 'Spice Army' means 'Crime Pays'!"

BRRRRRRP! BRRRRRP!

"I'll bet it's someone from Ace Department Store," Melissa said.

"Yeah," Sean said, grabbing the phone. "Or Electronics Alley." He spoke into the receiver. "Bloodhounds, Incorpora—oh . . . hi, Spalding."

"Spalding?" Melissa whispered. "What does he want?"

"You were?" Sean said. "Don't worry. We'll be right there."

"What's going on?" Melissa asked as Sean hung up the phone.

"Spalding's been arrested."

"Arrested? For what?"

"For breaking into the Midvale Diner."

9

Spalding Sings the Blues

SATURDAY, 10:29 PDST

Police Chief Robertson led Sean and Melissa down a long, white-tiled corridor. "I really didn't want to put him in a cell," he apologized. "But it's all I can do until we can get him over to juvenile hall."

"Have you called his parents?" Melissa asked.

The chief nodded. "His dad's out of town on a business trip, and his mom's busy with club meetings all day."

"You know, Chief Robertson," Sean said, "Spalding is innocent."

The chief sighed. "I know you guys are pretty good when it comes to solving crimes, but this time I'm afraid you're wrong. We caught him in the act."

"I didn't say he didn't do it," Sean replied. "I said he's innocent."

The chief chuckled. "I'm afraid you got me on that one. I'm clueless as to what you're saying."

Sean thought of explaining but figured it would take too long. He didn't have to worry. Melissa was already changing the subject.

"Speaking of being clueless," she asked, "about those two new cadets you hired . . ."

"You mean Bill and Phil?" the chief said. "My nephews?"

"Your neph—" Sean began.

"That's right." The chief nodded sadly. "My sister's kids. I know they're a little clumsy and overly eager, but they're gonna be just fine once they've had some experience." And then, under his breath, he added, "I hope."

Sean and Melissa looked doubtfully at each other.

"Anyway, here we are." Chief Robertson turned the key in the lock and the door creaked open. A moment later, Sean and Melissa were standing in Spalding's cell.

Spalding's eyes were red and so was his nose. It looked sore—like he'd blown it at least a hundred times. "I am so pleased to see you two!" he cried. *"HOOONK!"* (Make that 101 times.) "Can you deliver me from this institution?"

"We'll try," Sean said. "But tell us what happened."

"A young man, whom I have never laid eyes upon before, knocked upon my door and relayed to me that KC desperately needed to rendezvous with me at the Midvale Diner. He insisted the matter was quite urgent."

"And you believed him?" Melissa asked.

"He was quite convincing," Spalding said. "However, when I arrived at the diner, KC was nowhere to be seen. The diner was closed, but the front door to the establishment stood unlocked and wide open. I thought she might be in trouble there, so I went in. That is when the police arrived and proceeded to arrest me."

"And you told the police you were looking for a friend who might be in trouble?" Melissa asked.

"Precisely. However, they did not believe me. They insisted I was some sort of hoodlum simply by the way I'm dressed. *HONNNNKK!"* (Make that 102 times.) "I made it plain that my tattoos were simply painted on and that my body piercings were not real, but they chose not to believe me. They insisted that no respectable youngster would dress like this. And when they discovered the tongue stud in my pocket, they grew very excited. Somehow they deduced that I had been shooting at their two police officers."

KNOCK, KNOCK!

"You got another visitor, kid," an officer called. And then, to their alarm, Rafael Ruelas stepped in, followed by his cameraman!

"Which one of you is the criminal mastermind?" Ruelas asked.

Spalding protested, "I am not a criminal master—"

"And these must be some other members of your gang." He gestured at Sean and Melissa.

"No!" Melissa began. "We're just visi—"

"Are we ready?" Ruelas asked his cameraman. "How do I look? Is my hair okay?"

"You look terrific," the cameraman said.

"Wonderful! Wonderful! I'm ready for the stand-up interview." He sat next to Spalding (which was a strange way to do a stand-up interview) and began warming up his voice, "Mi mi mi mi mi mi mi!"

The cameraman counted down, "Three . . . two . . . one . . . rolling!"

Suddenly Ruelas was serious and intense. "The good citizens of Midvale will sleep easier tonight knowing that the mastermind of a sinister and violent gang of criminals is behind bars. . . ."

But Spalding sure didn't look like any kind of criminal mastermind. Instead, at the moment, he looked very small and sad and scared. Very, very scared.

SATURDAY, 11: 49 PDST

"What time is the final concert this afternoon?" Sean asked as he and Melissa headed back up Main Street.

"Two o'clock."

"That means we've got a little over two hours."

"To do what?" Melissa asked.

"I'm thinking! I'm thinking!" Sean answered.

"What's a scraped goat?" a squeaky voice suddenly asked.

Sean looked down at his watch. It was OutaSy—er . . . Jeremiah.

"*Scape*goat," Melissa corrected. "Not *scraped goat*. A scapegoat is someone who takes the blame for something he didn't do."

"Where'd you hear that word?" Sean asked.

"Well, I've been hanging out with the guys in Spice Army, and they've been laughing about someone who's acting as their scraped—er . . . scapegoat."

"Really?" Sean asked. "What else do they say?"

Jeremiah shrugged. "Not much. Just that they're using music to send messages to their gang. And that they've got something really big planned for Midvale State Bank this afternoon and—oh, you'll be happy to hear this—without KRZY radio, they couldn't be doing any of this."

Sean and Melissa went cold.

"They've . . . they've been using Dad's station for their plans?" Sean asked.

Jeremiah nodded. "You hit the nail right on

the foot. And this afternoon at the bank it's especially going to come in handy."

"Sean!" Melissa cried.

"I know, I know!" he answered. "They're going to rob the bank, and somehow they're going to use Dad's station to help! We've got to stop the broadcast!"

SATURDAY, 12:23 PDST

Sean and Melissa ran up the steps of the Midvale Police Department. The officer on duty had his nose stuck in a magazine.

"We need to see Chief Robertson," Melissa cried.

The officer slowly lowered the magazine to reveal he was—

"Officer Bill!" Sean exclaimed.

"Yes, may I help you?"

"We need to see Chief Robertson," Melissa repeated.

"I'm afraid that's impossible," Officer Bill said. "Uncle John—I mean the chief—has a case of the flu, so he went home with orders not to be disturbed."

"But, but, but—" Sean sputtered.

"We want to report a crime!" Melissa interrupted.

"I see . . ." The officer sounded anything but convinced. "And when and where did this crime take place?"

"It hasn't," Sean said. "Not yet. But it will. In a little over an hour."

Officer Bill sighed. "I'm sorry, but I'm far too busy to play your little game of cops and robbers."

"Call your uncle," Sean pleaded. "Please! He knows us. He'll tell you we're not lying."

"Sorry. The chief doesn't want to be bothered. Run along, now. And look both ways before crossing the street."

A moment later, the two were rushing out of the police station. "Where to now?" Melissa asked.

"The radio station! We've got to get Dad to call off that broadcast!"

"We'd better hurry," Melissa said, glancing at her watch. "We don't have much time!"

10

The Not-So-Grand Finale

SATURDAY, 13:04 PDST

Sean arrived at the radio station first and ran inside. "Dad! Dad!"

Herbie came from the control room. "Hey, Sean, what's up?"

"I gotta talk to Dad! He can't broadcast that concert!"

Melissa burst through the door. "Herbie!" Then turning to her brother, she asked, "Did you tell him?"

"What exactly is going on?" Herbie demanded.

"It's a long story and there's not much time," Sean said. "Get Dad and we'll explain."

Herbie shook his head. "Afraid I can't do that."

"But you have to!" Melissa exclaimed.

"Your dad's not here," Herbie said.

"What?"

"He had to go to Hurleyville on business. He won't be back until tonight."

"Then you can do it," Sean said. "Go on the air and say you can't broadcast the concert due to circumstances beyond your control."

"Guys," Herbie said, "I can't do that! Do you know how much money this station stands to make from this concert?"

"But if you don't—"

"I'm sorry. I can't do it without direct orders from your father."

"Then call him on his cell phone!" Sean urged.

Herbie shook his head. "He's in an important meeting with some potential advertisers. I can't bother him."

Sean and Melissa looked at each other, both thinking the same thing:

Now what?!

SATURDAY, 13:31 PDST

Midvale City Park Amphitheater was jam-packed, and the air was thick with excitement. Backstage, members of Spice Army were positive they were about to give Midvale a send-off they would never forget.

The drummer absentmindedly banged out a beat on the arm of his chair. "I wish we could get on with it," he said. "I'm getting kind of nervous."

The group's leader laughed. "Relax! There's nothing to be nervous about. A couple of hours from now and we'll be on our way out of town with a bazillion dollars in cold, hard cash!"

SATURDAY, 13:32 PDST

Back at the radio station, Melissa suddenly smiled her sweetest smile. "That's okay, Herbie," she said. "Thanks a lot, anyway."

"But . . ." Sean protested.

"We'll see you later," she said.

"But . . . but . . ."

109

Grabbing her brother's arm, she headed out the door. "Bye-bye . . ."

Once they were outside, Sean demanded, "What are you doing? We can't give up that easily!"

"I've got an idea," she replied.

"Which is. . . ?"

"We can pull the plug on the transmitter."

"Pull the plug on the. . . ? How are we gonna do that?"

"Together, that's how!"

Sean stole another glance at his watch. They had less than thirty minutes, and they had to do *something*.

"Okay," he finally sighed. "It's worth a try. Let's go!"

SATURDAY, 13:51 PDST

Doc sat in her laboratory, looking down at the paper in front of her. Before she called the authorities, she wanted to be sure she hadn't made any mistakes.

No. Her computations were correct. Whoever was responsible for these "messages from space" was planning an attack on Midvale State Bank . . . in just over nine minutes.

She reached over, picked up her text telephone, and hesitated. *What if the FBI doesn't believe me?* she thought.

SATURDAY, 13:58 PDST

Ever so quietly, Sean and Melissa reentered the station and sneaked into the transmitter room. They gritted their teeth and pulled and pulled on the transformer cord with all their might.

But nothing happened.

"It's no use!" Sean exclaimed. "It won't budge."

He looked down at his hands, which were red and raw from pulling so hard.

"We can't give up," Melissa said. "We need to keep yanking."

Sean shook his head. "We gotta think of another way."

Melissa looked at her watch. "The concert is already starting!" she said. "We don't have time to do anything else. Let's give it another try!"

With a heavy sigh, Sean nodded. "All right . . ."

He and Melissa both grabbed hold.

"Okay," he said. "On three. One, two . . . pull!"

"NGGGHH!" They pulled with all of their might. Their muscles strained and their faces reddened until finally:

KER-PLOP!

Success!

The cord pulled out and lay lifeless on the ground. The transmitter was dead . . . at least temporarily.

"We made it!" Melissa shouted.

Sean glanced at his watch. "I'm not so sure."

"So what do we do next?"

"We'd better get over to the Midvale State Bank."

"No way," Melissa said. "We're not going over to that bank by ourselves and do battle with a bunch of criminals."

"Misty?"

"Huh-uh, no way."

"Okay, then, we'll get some help."

"That's better."

He turned and started for the door. Melissa followed. "But who?" she asked, running to keep up. "Who are we getting to help?"

"Why, Slobs, of course."

"Sean . . ."

SATURDAY, 14:18 PDST

Slobs barked ferociously as she led Sean and Melissa down Main Street. The bank lay just ahead.

"I don't see any robbers," Melissa shouted over the roar of her scooter and her brother's skateboard.

"Maybe we got the plug pulled in time!" Sean shouted back. *Or maybe we were wrong about the whole thing*, he thought.

They came to a stop in the bank parking lot, and both let out a heavy sigh. There was only a bunch of ordinary townspeople going about their ordinary business, carrying big bags of ordinary money in and out—

Wait a minute! Big bags of money!

Those weren't ordinary citizens! They were bank robbers! A half dozen of them!

"Sean," Melissa whispered, "do something!"

"Like what? There are too many of them!"

"Well, if you won't, I will!"

Before Sean could stop her, Melissa climbed up on the hood of a nearby car. "You're all under arrest!" she shouted.

Everyone froze a minute . . . until they saw Melissa standing there. Then they all broke out laughing.

"I said, you're under arrest!" she shouted.

Realizing he had to help, Sean reluctantly climbed up on the car beside her. "That's right!" he shouted. "Now, set those sacks of money down and put your hands in the air!"

"Hey, look, everybody!" one of the robbers shouted. "We're being arrested by two little kids and—" he pointed to Slobs—"and a Chihuahua!"

"GRRRRRR!" (You can imagine Slobs wasn't too keen on being mistaken for a Chihuahua.)

114

"Don't worry," another shouted. "they're just a couple of flies in the ointment, and we all know what to do with flies! Right, boys?"

"That's right," another shouted as he started toward them. "You squash them!" The others agreed and started to move in.

"WOOF! WOOF! WOOF! WOOF!" Slobs let out a flurry of barks, bracing herself, getting ready to protect her owners with her very life. But there were so many of them! And now they were slowly surrounding the kids . . . closing in.

"GRRRRRRRR!"

Suddenly one of the robbers produced a crowbar and headed straight toward Slobs.

"Slobs, look out!" Sean yelled.

Slobs spun around. "WOOF! WOOF! WOOF! WOOF!" She was barking so furiously she stopped the man in his tracks. And then they heard it.

WAAAAAAAAAAA!

A siren. A police siren. That was the good news. Unfortunately, there was a little bad news. It was Phil and Bill! They hit their . . .

SCREEEETCH!

115

. . . brakes, but just a few seconds too late, which caused them to . . .

KEEERASH!

. . . into a tree, which . . .

PFFFFFTTTTT!

. . . inflated their air bags, trapping both of them in their car, which . . .

"Har . . . har . . . har . . ."

. . . caused all the robbers to bust a gut laughing. But only for a second, because suddenly . . .

WAAAAAAAAA!

. . . there were more sirens! About a half dozen Midvale police cars flew around the corner, screeching to a halt in front of the bank.

Twelve uniformed officers jumped out with their guns drawn.

"Get your hands up where we can see them!" one of the policemen yelled.

The crooks had no option but to obey . . . just as another car zipped around the corner and skidded to a halt.

"It's Dad!" Sean shouted.

"And Chief Robertson!" Melissa exclaimed.

While the other officers rounded up the criminals, Sean and Melissa ran to their father.

"How did you know?" Sean asked.

"I was in this meeting," Dad said, "and I don't know how it happened, but all of a sudden, this voice started coming through my laptop. A really strange electrical voice."

Sean and Melissa exchanged looks. *Jeremiah!*

"And he convinced me you guys were in trouble. Then he told me I had to get to Midvale State Bank right away."

"Same thing happened to me," Chief Robertson said. "Only it was on my TV at home. And he was green and big and—" lowering his voice, he glanced around—"kinda ugly."

"What about Spice Army?" Sean asked.

"Someone called the FBI," Chief Robertson stated. "Bank robbery's a federal crime, you know."

Dad nodded. "They'll be arrested as soon as they walk off the stage."

Just then, the chief noticed Bill and Phil struggling to get out from underneath their air bags. "Oh man . . ." he sighed. "The things I do for my sister. I guess I'd better go see if I can get them out of there." And with another heavy sigh, he headed over to help his bungling nephews.

With a big grin, Dad turned back to Sean and Melissa. "Congratulations, you guys," he said. "Looks like Bloodhounds, Incorporated, has done it again. I'm really proud of you!"

Sean and Melissa traded looks and broke into big grins.

"Come here, you two." Dad held out his arms, and they moved into a three-way group hug.

"WOOF! WOOF! WOOF!"

Er . . . make that a four-way group hug . . . with drool.

"SLOBS!"

Lots and lots of drool. It's a bloodhound specialty.

MONDAY, 7 : 30 PDST
(FIRST DAY OF SCHOOL)

"Hey, guys!"

Spalding was waiting for Sean and Melissa in

118

front of Midvale Middle School.

"I wish to express my extreme gratitude for you removing me from the hot water I was in."

"No sweat!" Sean said.

"You're welcome," Melissa agreed.

"May I ask you what you plan to do with the reward money the bank gave you?"

"Donate it to our favorite radio station." Sean smiled.

"So," Spalding said, "explain it to me again. Those guys were . . ."

"Broadcasting a super-high frequency through the radio station," Sean said.

"Which our friend thought were messages from another planet, but which were really used to unlock locks and turn off alarms all around town."

"And," Sean added, "they were also sending out coded messages in their lyrics during their concerts to tell their partners in crime which stores to practice on."

"Practice?" Spalding asked.

"Exactly," Melissa said. "That's why they never stole anything . . . well, except for those

119

few textbooks to make it look like you were the culprit."

"That is why they had me go to the diner?" Spalding asked.

"Yup." Melissa nodded. "They wanted to make you the scapegoat. That's also why they stole your monogrammed tongue studs and planted them at the break-ins."

"That's right," Sean said. "And with all your tattoos and body piercings, you fit the bill perfectly."

Spalding looked down at the ground and let out a long, low sigh. "I believe I have certainly learned my lesson on this one," he said.

"Let's hope so," Sean said.

" 'Abstain from all appearance of evil,' " Melissa quoted.

"What's that?"

"It's from the Bible," she said.

Spalding nodded. "Well, it certainly makes an extreme amount of sense."

"Hey, guys!"

They looked up to see KC and Bear approaching.

"Check it out." KC handed them a flyer. "It's a

brand-new band coming to town. They're performing this Saturday."

"Thanks," Sean said, taking the flyer.

"So, Spalding, you gonna help me with my homework this year?" KC demanded.

"Don't I always?"

"You'd better!"

With that, the threesome shuffled off, leaving Sean and Melissa to themselves.

"Well, another case solved," Sean said.

"And another lesson learned," Melissa added.

"Yeah," Sean said. He looked at the flyer. "This band looks kinda cool."

Melissa nodded as she looked over his shoulder. Suddenly she let out a groan. "Oh no!"

"What's wrong?"

"Look at the name of the band."

Sean glanced back at the flyer. "I think it's great. What's wrong with 'Aliens Shave Dirt'?"

Melissa grabbed a pencil from her pocket and quickly began to rearrange the letters. "Nothing" she said. "Absolutely nothing. Then again, maybe everything."

"What do you mean?" Sean said. Then, looking at her paper, it was his turn to let out a groan. For, there on the flyer, his sister had just rearranged the letters of Aliens Shave Dirt to read, "Thieves and Liars."

"Great," he sighed, "just great."

"Buckle in, big brother," Melissa giggled. "Bloodhounds, Incorporated, just might wind up with another big case. . . ."

By Bill Myers

Children's Series:
Bloodhounds, Inc. — mystery/comedy
McGee and Me! — book and video
The Incredible Worlds of Wally McDoogle — comedy

Teen Series:
Forbidden Doors

Adult Novels:
Blood of Heaven
Threshold
Fire of Heaven
Eli
When the Last Leaf Falls

Nonfiction:
The Dark Side of the Supernatural
Hot Topics, Tough Questions
Faith Encounter
Just Believe It

Picture Books:
Baseball for Breakfast

Seeking Excitement and Adventure?

Have you ever missed your family? Or wanted nothing more than to be home? You'll identify with Robert Elmer's characters in his PROMISE OF ZION series. Dov is a thirteen-year-old separated from his family by WWII who dreams of being reunited with them. Emily, the thirteen-year-old daughter of a British official, is finding it hard to be away from her home in England. As the world about them is thrown into chaos with the Jewish people trying to reestablish their home in Israel, the two become friends and try to help each other fulfill their ultimate dreams.

Promise Breaker by Robert Elmer
Peace Rebel • Refugee Treasure • Brother Enemy • Freedom Trap

Good-hearted and inquisitive, Mandie is growing up in the early 1900s. Her adventures will take you to a world you've never visited. Together with her kitten, Snowball, Mandie and her friends have fun solving mysteries.

MANDIE BOOKS by Lois Gladys Leppard

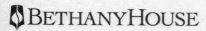